WISCONSIN

Sarah Tieck

Big Buddy BOOKS
Explore the United States

VISIT US AT
www.abdopublishing.com

Published by ABDO Publishing Company, PO Box 398166, Minneapolis, MN 55439.

Printed in the United States of America, North Mankato, Minnesota.
062012
092012

  PRINTED ON RECYCLED PAPER

Coordinating Series Editor: Rochelle Baltzer
Contributing Editors: Megan M. Gunderson, Marcia Zappa
Graphic Design: Adam Craven
Cover Photograph: *iStockphoto*: ©iStockphoto.com/steverts.
Interior Photographs/Illustrations: *AP Photo*: AP Photo (p. 25), AP Photo, File (p. 23), Morry Gash (p. 23), Morry Gash, File (p. 19), Casey Lake (p. 19), North Wind Picture Archives via AP Images (p. 13), Wisconsin State Journal, Sarah B. Tews (p. 27); *Getty Images*: Paul Drinkwater/NBC/NBCU Photo Bank via Getty Images (p. 26), Tom Hollyman/Photo Researchers (p. 21), Independent Picture Service/UIG via Getty Images (p. 26); *iStockphoto*: ©iStockphoto.com/benkrut (p. 11), ©iStockphoto.com/dlewis33 (p. 27), ©iStockphoto.com/filo (p. 30), ©iStockphoto.com/timhughes (p. 9), ©iStockphoto.com/lightstalker (p. 5), ©iStockphoto.com/YinYang (p. 29); *Shutterstock*: John Brueske (p. 17), Melinda Fawver (p. 30), Mark Herreid (p. 27), Philip Lange (p. 30), Henryk Sadura (p. 11), gregg williams (p. 30).

All population figures taken from the 2010 US census.

Library of Congress Cataloging-in-Publication Data

Tieck, Sarah, 1976-
  Wisconsin / Sarah Tieck.
      p. cm. -- (Explore the United States)
  ISBN 978-1-61783-389-2
  1. Wisconsin--Juvenile literature. I. Title.
  F581.3.T54 2013
  977.5--dc23
                              2012018274

Contents

ONE NATION

The United States is a **diverse** country. It has farmland, cities, coasts, and mountains. Its people come from many different backgrounds. And, its history covers more than 200 years.

Today the country includes 50 states. Wisconsin is one of these states. Let's learn more about this state and its story!

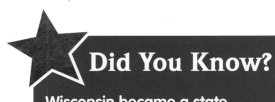

Did You Know?

Wisconsin became a state on May 29, 1848. It was the thirtieth state to join the nation.

Wisconsin is known for its dairy farms. It is often called "America's Dairyland."

WISCONSIN UP CLOSE

The United States has four main **regions**. Wisconsin is in the Midwest.

Wisconsin has four states on its borders. Michigan is northeast. Illinois is south. Iowa and Minnesota are west.

Wisconsin has a total area of 65,496 square miles (169,634 sq km). About 5.7 million people live there.

REGIONS OF THE UNITED STATES

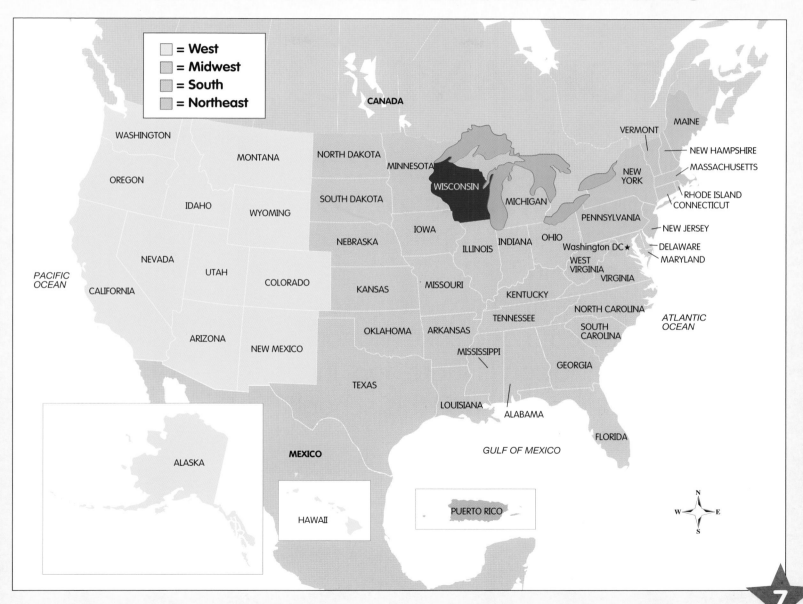

= West
= Midwest
= South
= Northeast

CANADA

WASHINGTON
MONTANA
NORTH DAKOTA
MINNESOTA
OREGON
IDAHO
WYOMING
SOUTH DAKOTA
WISCONSIN
MICHIGAN
VERMONT
MAINE
NEW HAMPSHIRE
MASSACHUSETTS
NEW YORK
RHODE ISLAND
CONNECTICUT
PENNSYLVANIA
NEW JERSEY
IOWA
NEBRASKA
ILLINOIS
INDIANA
OHIO
Washington DC★
DELAWARE
MARYLAND
NEVADA
UTAH
COLORADO
WEST VIRGINIA
VIRGINIA
PACIFIC OCEAN
CALIFORNIA
KANSAS
MISSOURI
KENTUCKY
NORTH CAROLINA
ATLANTIC OCEAN
ARIZONA
NEW MEXICO
OKLAHOMA
ARKANSAS
TENNESSEE
SOUTH CAROLINA
MISSISSIPPI
GEORGIA
TEXAS
LOUISIANA
ALABAMA
FLORIDA
GULF OF MEXICO
MEXICO
ALASKA
HAWAII
PUERTO RICO

N
W E
S

7

IMPORTANT CITIES

Madison is Wisconsin's **capital**. It is also the second-largest city in the state. Madison is home to 233,209 people. It has been the capital since Wisconsin became a state in 1848.

Madison is located between two large lakes. These are Lake Mendota and Lake Monona. The University of Wisconsin–Madison is there, too. In 2012, more than 40,000 students attended this school!

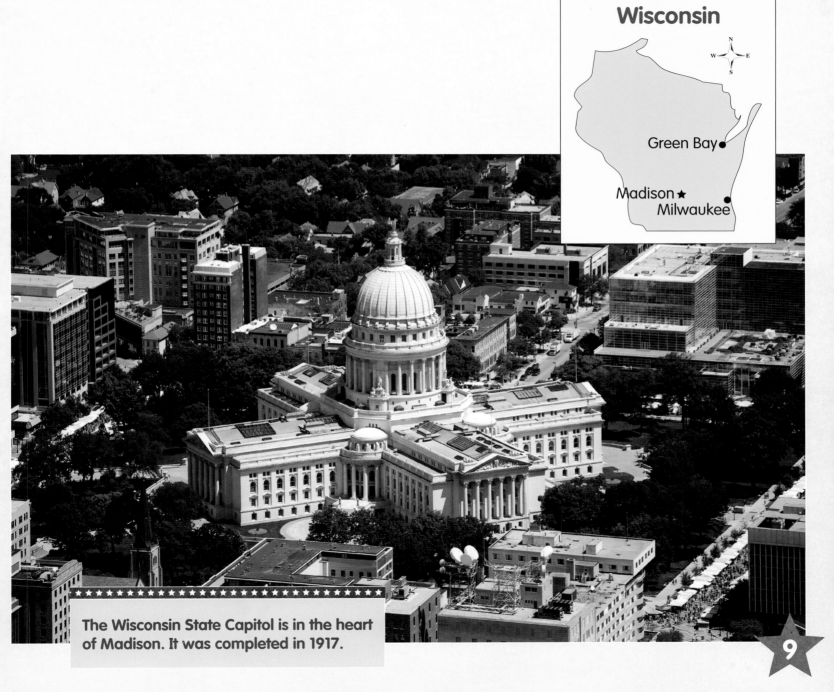

Wisconsin

Green Bay

Madison ★
Milwaukee

The Wisconsin State Capitol is in the heart
of Madison. It was completed in 1917.

Milwaukee (mihl-WAW-kee) is Wisconsin's largest city. It is home to 594,833 people. It is known for manufacturing products such as machinery and foods. The Milwaukee River flows through this city.

Green Bay is the third-largest city in the state. It has 104,057 people. It is home to the Green Bay Packers football team. This team is owned by community members. So, it has many fans in Green Bay.

Milwaukee is on the shores of Lake Michigan.

The Green Bay Packers play at Lambeau Field in Green Bay.

WISCONSIN IN HISTORY

Wisconsin's history includes Native Americans, explorers, and settlers. In 1634, the first known French explorers visited what is now Wisconsin. They met Native Americans, who had lived there for thousands of years.

Over time, more explorers and settlers arrived. The Wisconsin Territory was created in 1836. In 1848, Wisconsin became a state.

In 1673, Jacques Marquette and Louis Jolliet explored Wisconsin's rivers.

Timeline

1854

Meetings in Wisconsin led to the start of the Republican Party. This party became one of two major US political parties.

1871

A forest fire burned Peshtigo and the surrounding area in northeastern Wisconsin. About 1,200 people died.

1836

The Wisconsin Territory was created.

1800s

Wisconsin became the thirtieth state.

1848

The first US kindergarten was opened in Watertown by Margaretha Meyer Schurz.

William Horlick of Racine invented malted milk.

1887

1856

1959

Vince Lombardi became the head coach of the Green Bay Packers football team.

2011

The University of Wisconsin–Madison Badgers football team won the Big Ten Conference.

1900s

2000s

The Green Bay Packers won the first Super Bowl.

1967

Eric Heiden of Madison took part in the Winter Olympics. He set a record by winning five gold medals in speed skating.

1980

15

ACROSS THE LAND

Wisconsin has hills, valleys, cliffs, forests, lakes, and rivers. The Wisconsin River flows through the state. Also, two of the Great Lakes touch Wisconsin. Lake Michigan forms the state's eastern border. Lake Superior is north.

Many types of animals make their homes in Wisconsin. These include beavers, badgers, coyotes, and deer.

Did You Know?

In July, the average temperature in Wisconsin is 70°F (21°C). In January, it is 14°F (-10°C).

Big Manitou Falls on the Black River is the state's highest waterfall. It drops down about 165 feet (50 m)!

17

EARNING A LIVING

Wisconsin has many important businesses. Some people have service jobs, such as working in banks or helping visitors to the state. Others work in factories that make dairy foods or paper.

Wisconsin has many natural **resources**. Its forests provide timber. Sand and gravel come from the state's mines. Farmers produce dairy products, beef cattle, corn, cranberries, and snap beans.

Wisconsin is known for producing dairy products. These include cheese (*right*), milk, and butter.

MOTOR
HARLEY-DAVIDSON
COMPANY®

Harley-Davidson motorcycles are made in Milwaukee.

19

Natural Wonder

The Wisconsin Dells is an area on the Wisconsin River. The river flows through a **canyon** with rock formations and sandstone cliffs. This land was shaped over thousands of years by melting **glaciers**.

Today, the Wisconsin Dells is a popular vacation spot. It is known for its natural beauty. There are also water parks, boat rides, live shows, and amusement parks.

People often view the rock cliffs from boats.

HOMETOWN HEROES

Many famous people have lived in Wisconsin. **Architect** Frank Lloyd Wright was born in Richland Center in 1867. He was known for creating long, low buildings that blend in with the land. This is called prairie style.

Wright's work is known all over the world. One of his famous buildings is the Guggenheim Museum in New York City, New York. Another is the Fallingwater house in Mill Run, Pennsylvania.

Taliesin is in Spring Green. It was Wright's home and is one of his most famous buildings.

Wright's style has been used by other architects.

23

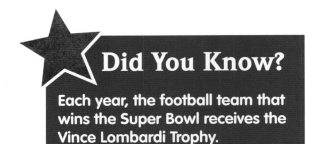

Did You Know?

Each year, the football team that wins the Super Bowl receives the Vince Lombardi Trophy.

Vince Lombardi was born in New York City, New York, in 1913. He was famous for his part in Wisconsin sports. Lombardi was the head coach of the Green Bay Packers from 1959 to 1968. He was honored by the Pro Football Hall of Fame in 1971.

Lombardi was known for his team pride and for pushing his players. He coached the Packers when they won the first two Super Bowls.

25

Tour Book

Do you want to go to Wisconsin? If you visit the state, here are some places to go and things to do!

 **Taste**

Eat some fried cheese curds. Wisconsin is famous for these tasty dairy treats!

 **See**

Visit the House on the Rock in Spring Green. It is known for its unusual rooms and displays. It has 22 rooms!

 Discover

Camp or kayak around the Apostle Islands. These are in northern Wisconsin in Lake Superior.

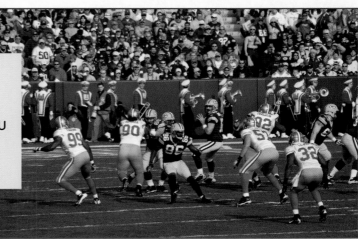

Cheer

See the Green Bay Packers play at Lambeau Field. This field is outside, so some games are played in the snow and cold!

Remember

Learn about the history of the circus in Baraboo. Circus World Museum has objects from the Ringling Brothers Circus, which began there in 1884.

A GREAT STATE

The story of Wisconsin is important to the United States. The people and places that make up this state offer something special to the country. Together with all the states, Wisconsin helps make the United States great.

Door County is located in eastern Wisconsin on Lake Michigan. It is known for its lighthouses.

Fast Facts

Date of Statehood:
May 29, 1848

Population (rank):
5,686,986
(20th most-populated state)

Total Area (rank):
65,496 square miles
(22nd largest state)

Motto:
"Forward"

Nickname:
Badger State,
America's Dairyland

State Capital:
Madison

Flag:

Flower: Wood Violet

Postal Abbreviation:
WI

Tree: Sugar Maple

Bird: American Robin

Important Words

architect (AHR-kuh-tehkt) a person who designs buildings, bridges, and other things.

canyon a long, narrow valley between two cliffs.

capital a city where government leaders meet.

diverse made up of things that are different from each other.

glacier (GLAY-shuhr) a huge chunk of ice and snow on land.

region a large part of a country that is different from other parts.

resource a supply of something useful or valued.

Web Sites

To learn more about Wisconsin, visit ABDO Publishing Company online. Web sites about Wisconsin are featured on our Book Links page. These links are routinely monitored and updated to provide the most current information available.

www.abdopublishing.com

Index